THE DISINVENT MOVEMENT

THE DISINVENT MOVEMENT

Susanna Gendall

Victoria University of Wellington Press

Victoria University of Wellington Press
PO Box 600, Wellington
New Zealand
vup.wgtn.ac.nz

A catalogue record is available from the
National Library of New Zealand.

ISBN 9781776564101

Published with the assistance of a grant from

Printed in Singapore by Markono Print Media Pte Ltd

'Modernity's history is also a history of four centuries of cultural and physical genocide in the name of an imaginary unitary society.'

Abdullah Öcalan

The Disinvent Movement

I had to go to the doctor. He was interested in the shape of the wound on my forehead, which he thought resembled a letter in Arabic. Arabic was his maternal language and he thought it was unfortunate that it had a reputation for being an ugly language when in fact it was very beautiful. He recited a poem for me in Arabic about the rain.

'Do you see?' he said. 'Can you hear?'

'I can.'

'Keep still,' he said.

He was less interested in how I got the wound, but I told him anyway as I'd spent all morning rehearsing.

'You see, I always go to the swimming pool on Thursday mornings, but when I got there I found that I'd forgotten my jandals.'

'Ah yes, and you slipped.'

I liked how eager he was to conspire with me.

'I slipped right next to the children's pool where those bars stick out – you know? I guess I hit a sharp edge on my way down.'

He didn't want to talk about accidents anymore. He wanted to talk about French swimming pools and how much he hated them, how slippery the floors were and how he couldn't stand all that nonsense about compulsory bathing caps – and what on earth were all those shallow heavily chlorinated pools that one had to wade through to access the main swimming pool? It was like being in wartime again. He'd seen it a thousand times – people slipping over on those ridiculous floors. This was the first time, however, that he'd seen such an exquisitely shaped result.

'Would you mind if I took a photo?' he said.

I didn't mind.

He said that unfortunately it looked like I would need stitches.

'We could try a steri-strip.' He walked over to his desk and opened a drawer as if he might just happen to have one on him.

I asked him what a steri-strip was. I had been a good student and knew when to ask a question.

He told me that it was a piece of adhesive gauze that encouraged two pieces of separated skin to knit together again. It made me think of the North Island and the South Island, which I'd heard were imperceptibly moving closer to each other. He returned from the drawer empty-handed and peered into the cut.

'But this one looks as if it will need some help from the outside.'

He produced two packages, which he ripped open with his teeth. I inhaled the coffee on his breath as he dabbed something yellow over the cut. To my surprise, he began to thread an actual needle. I'd always assumed 'stitches' was a metaphor for something else. It had not occurred to me that a person could be sewn up like a doll. When my mother had sewn up a doll whose head had become detached from her body, she had drawn attention to the neutral expression on the doll's face to prove that it didn't hurt her. I focussed on keeping my face blank as the doctor sewed five stitches into my forehead. He told me on the way out that if I must go to the swimming pool I should always remember my jandals. There were many varieties of fungal infection at those French swimming pools that were just waiting to be picked up.

2

How does one get in?

There was the squash playing. The squash court was inside a large windowless building of which the entrance itself had been particularly hard to find. If only it was as easy as finding a doorway. The real problem was once you were inside alone with the squash balls and squash rackets on the squash court. I thought this was going to be a good place for me – it was cool and dark and there were no teams or uniforms or girls who demanded you pass them the ball. And when people asked me what I'd been doing all afternoon I could say, 'I've been playing squash.'

But squash did not want me to play with it. I kept swinging my racket but the ball dodged it. I did not take my eyes off the ball. The more I watched it the less I hit it. After a while it began to feel like a conspiracy between the racket and the ball to keep me out. It was an awesome feeling to build up so much hate for something. The man told my mother that my imagination was proving problematic and that I should come back in six months once I'd settled down. He thought I was intentionally keeping myself out. 'There's a door,' he said, 'but she's decided not to walk through it.'

3

There was that time I looked around and noticed that everyone else had crossed over to the other side. I had no idea where they were or how they got there – all I knew was that I was not with them. It looked so picturesque over there. They all had bras on and were sharing private jokes. I made several attempts at crashing on through, but like with everything there was a proper way to go about things. I had to walk through the front door just as they had. For a brief infantile moment I thought that they had simply forgotten me, and I waited patiently like the goat in that story for someone to come back and get me.

This was not that story.

4

Every day it was the same scene: the bus, the field and the different constellations dotted across the field like a whole cosmos that you could only access through a telescope. I wondered if you could get confined in childhood forever – the same way adults get confined in adulthood – and be unable to proceed instead of unable to return. In the end I sat it out in the toilets and waited for the present to end.

I don't know if it ever did. I realised this recently when I found myself in a hot meeting room with eleven teachers and a blue-eyed principal in a high school in the ninth arrondissement of Paris. Although I understood most of what they were saying, and in theory I spoke French, their faces revealed layers and layers of perplexity every time I opened my mouth. Language was clearly not the partner in crime I had been led to believe it was. Language had fuck-all to do with it. It was very unladylike to say fuck-all in French – even the filmmaker who lived across the road and liked to dress up as Wonder Woman never did it. There was a moment of silence in the meeting room, and I realised I had been naïve. The way in was somewhere much deeper. It was buried. You had to go through subterranean tunnels to find it, like the tunnels I'd been told still existed under the school, accessible through trapdoors that could be found in the boys' toilets. You basically had to bury yourself alive if you ever wanted to find them.

5

I joined a gym for a while. I must have been twelve. My friend Asher already went and she suggested we go to the aerobics class together. Plus there was a café downstairs where you could go and drink banana and berry smoothies afterwards. The aerobics class was harder than we'd thought it would be. Everyone had their own wooden block that they had to step on and off. It was a revolution in aerobics. We were surrounded by a sea of grown-ups and the music was horrible, but it was wonderful to be part of something that made no sense. Afterwards at the café I asked Asher if she thought I was different, if she had noticed that I didn't seem like myself. She sucked harder on the straw to free the wedge of frozen banana that had got stuck there. She had no idea what I was going on about, but now that I said it, yes, I had been acting a bit weird today. Like how? Like how you asked that lady next to us in the changing rooms where she got her sweat band. That was not what I was talking about. But I admired Asher's consistency. I longed to be someone like her – someone who could manage to sustain a personality.

6

It's not exactly an original problem. Everyone is trying to get in. Look at all the photos. The people just about killing themselves trying to get across the English Channel, or trying to cross an invisible line that divides one piece of land from another. Every day they come up with a new tactic – hiding in trucks, changing their names or ages or origins. One guy was pulled out of the sea as he tried to swim across. People like him might have been awarded prestigious prizes for creativity. Instead they were returned to the place where they'd started. They were sent back to the beginning as if it was just a game of Snakes and Ladders we were all playing. Maybe that explained why some of them decided to quit. I was walking through the tunnels the other day, and I found a whole family living there. A little girl in a red dress was skipping, doing a perfect imitation of carefree existence underground.

7

I tried to be a teacher for a while. This seemed like an easy way in, or a good place to hide. I liked the complicit smiles and the way money appeared in your bank account on the same day every month. There was a staffroom with maps on the walls so that you would always have something to talk about. How many times did I point up to the green splodge located just above the coffee machine and say, 'That is where I was born.'

'Hold on, just let me get my glasses,' someone usually said. Many of them found it hard to understand what I was talking about without assistance. Something nearly always happened before they got around to finding their glasses – the bell went or another teacher intervened with an important question or the subject of the weather could not be put off any longer.

'You'll show us next time,' they said in the sing-song way they must have learned at teachers' college, their voices full of the promise of continuity and rewards. One lesson led to the next in a rational succession that led to a meaningful whole; each lesson related to the previous and the subsequent. Each was a chapter that summarised what had come before and enticed you on to what was yet to come. The re-cap, the warm-up, the in-tro, the re-vise, the con-clu – this was the sequence that was unerringly followed. I never got round to showing anyone where I was born. It was rare that I ran into the same person twice.

The students, however, sniffed me out straight away. They could see that I was no writer of chapters, that there would never be a book at the end. They knew that I didn't know if I was one of them or one of us. I kept asking them to rip pages out of their notebooks, for Christ's sake. How could continuity claim to exist in such a classroom? Yet when I glanced in the mirror between nine and ten and saw the touch of make-up and the dress, I looked a convincing enough insider. I purposefully wore those high-heels that made an authoritative clack as I approached the classroom. It was only when I took my place in front of the blackboard that childhood let me know who was in charge.

I wondered if they would keep my secret safe, and outside the classroom it appeared they were willing. They greeted me in corridors and meeting rooms and other ambivalent spaces as if I were indeed their teacher. It was only back in the classroom, where we could relax and be ourselves, that things became awkward. They didn't give a shit about what anyone else thought. They just wanted to make sure that I knew they knew.

I knew.

8

I met a tall man at a party. He was looking for whisky. He was conspicuously from LA – the height, the tan, the teeth, the complaints about the traffic. It took a while, but we finally got down to his beliefs.

He told me we were living in some kind of reproductive system and that we were constantly trying to be born, but that most of us would never reach that goal.

'You mean, we're sperm?'

'Basically,' he said.

It sounded like he'd been in France too long.

I led him down the corridor into the kitchen and we opened and closed all the cupboards, revealing a different kind of host from the one we knew. The tidy cans of corn and packets of rice had a temporary sobering effect as we witnessed the evidence of careful budgeting, and we were both a little embarrassed at seeing each other see who our host was when she was alone.

'What happens to those who do succeed?' I asked him.

'I guess they get born,' he said, 'but I've never met anyone that did that.'

We finally found a quarter bottle of whisky in a cabinet under the sink in the bathroom.

'Trust the French. They use it as mouthwash.'

He calmed down after the whisky. He said he liked living in a foreign country because you had no idea what the fuck was going on. In LA he knew exactly what was going on. He used to get up every morning and drive down to the café and say, 'How's it going?' and he knew he would never get an answer. In another country it was like trying to crack a code. Most people leave because they can't crack it – or they can't be bothered. I asked him what he'd do once he'd cracked it. He bared his big white teeth once again in an outburst of arbitrary laughter.

'I'll never crack it. I'm not too worried about that.'

My neck was getting sore from looking up at him.

9

I met an environmental activist in a bar. He gave me my first driving lesson. Environmental activists still drove cars in those days. He offered me a lift home, but when we got to the car he changed his mind and asked me if I could drive instead; he'd had one too many tequilas.

'Don't worry,' he said. 'Three in the morning is a great time to learn.'

There were no cars on the streets, and the headlamps lit up the markings in bright yellow. We drove so slowly he had time to call out the name of every shop we passed. When we got to my flat he asked if he could sleep at my place.

I'm not sure if we slept.

He took my number but he never used it. It was hard to choose whether to go out and risk seeing him around or stay home and risk the phone ringing. I stayed home. I had a beautiful view of a volcano that no one ever really believed would erupt. Views had not yet been commoditised – they were either there or not there. Some time later I went out. Sometimes I had to get away from the phone not ringing. I walked all the way to the end of my street without running into anybody. When I got back my flatmate told me the phone had rung. He'd been in the bath and couldn't be bothered answering it. In the end, the environmental activist drove his car over. That was before cellphones.

I met this guy who spent half his life wearing a suit in America and the other half a mundu in Kerala. He was trying to work out what to do next. In the meantime he wore shirts and pants. He gave out business cards that said *consultant* in blue silky lettering. We drank faloodas and ate omelettes, and a little while later we took a train. Then we took a boat. There was a second-hand bookshop with no shelves, only piles and piles of books all the way up to the ceiling, violating all the rules of alphabetical ordering. The owner was the only one who could tell you where the book you wanted was. He was the only one who knew the way in. The consultant bought a book called *Three Men in a Boat* by Jerome K. Jerome. We laughed about it. Later I found what resembled a poem folded between pages 51 and 52.

II

I met Eric. He was sleeping on the bunk above mine in London. He had to leave the other place he was staying because the guy below him snored so loud he hadn't slept for the last ten days. We walked downstairs to the kitchen, where there were free cornflakes if you managed to get up before nine. He couldn't understand how something like a cornflake had been invented, especially as a food you would eat before nine o'clock. I sprinkled some sugar on mine to show him to what degree a bit of ground-down old corn could be revolutionised. He was unconvinced. 'Have you ever heard,' he asked me, 'of a croissant?'

'I have to go to work now,' I said, and he walked with me down the stairs and down the street and down into the tube, and off the tube and through Soho and into the pub where I worked. I wasn't sure about him. His parents weren't sure about him either. He wanted to be a musician but he told them he wanted to be an English teacher for the sake of argument, although, he said, you have to be careful about what you say you want. That was exactly how he had found himself in London.

Later, when we reversed roles and I went to see him in Metz, things were different. I was out, and he was in. There was a great big dictionary he kept by the door that we used in emergencies, of which there were many. His parents turned up one morning to check on their English teacher, and I escaped out the back door in size forty-five white sneakers and someone's black coat. It was four degrees outside and I wandered through a bleak landscape that seemed unsure about its fate as an urban suburb. Certain overgrown banks suggested revolt. Eric wrote something in French in my notebook when I left. *On se referme sur le but ultime, celui qui n'existe pas mais dont on se souvient trop souvent.*

'We'll meet again,' he said at the train station. We didn't.

I met my husband at the airport. I recognised him for what he was: my absolute negative. He told me the only reason he had come was because his colleague had broken her leg. I drove straight to the hotel and left him there. We didn't get around to talking until the day before he was due to leave. I can't remember what he said. He resembled a child as he sulked into his coffee cup, making patterns with the undissolved sugar grains he had discovered in the bottom of his cup. I was the mother and asked him what was wrong. Until now I had been surrounded by warmth and sunlight and noise, and this abrupt exit into shadow was almost thrilling. What *was* wrong? He couldn't tell me. It was all so complicated. I persisted, asking him variations of the same question as if it were just a matter of getting the password right, the same letters but in the correct order. He ordered more coffee, which only made him more reticent. Several weeks later I received a package in the mail. Inside the brown paper wrapping was a book with several crosses on the blank page before the story began. In the place I was living, it was rare for packages that were sent to ever arrive.

13

I met the man of my dreams.

The man in my dreams.

There were so many small words that meant so much.

I didn't recognise him at first. I'd always assumed he was a myth. He was strutting around a YouTube video in a suit and beard that kept his face a secret. He was talking to us about a bright, modern painting that meant a lot to him. He made frequent eye contact with his audience, being careful not to look at his notes too often. Although there were one thousand, six hundred and seventy-four of us, I noticed he made a special effort to look in my direction. It was funny to bump into him here, when there were so many other pages and places we might have been, people we could have ended up as. I wondered if he had met me on the internet before as I was now meeting him, if I had turned up unannounced in his dreams as he had turned up in mine. Earlier that morning, I'd met him without the beard or the suit. I put an amethyst stone in his hand to let him know how I felt about him. Real life was a luxury now and we had to make do with what we could. I'd heard that due to advances in modern medicine and improved sanitation, there were too many people in the world. Instead of one thousand, six hundred and seventy-four, there might have been only five hundred and nineteen. Instead of five hundred and nineteen there might have been thirty-seven. Instead of thirty-seven, there might have been just the two of us, alone on the internet.

'You should be more like the Chinese restaurant on the corner,' someone said. I think it was my mother. Before it was a Chinese restaurant it was a Lebanese place with heavy purple curtains. Like every restaurant on the corner, it had shut down after a while. The curtains remained pulled for three months. The ornamental gold lettering was scratched off the window, letter by letter. A big white panel revealing flashing electric letters appeared one morning. *Realm of Asia*, it said. I admired the name. It suggested so much and so little, precise yet vague, an approximation, a refusal to be shut in, pinned down, wrapped up. It could mean anything really.

More time went by. My uncle came to visit with his young girlfriend. He was an exact replica of my dead grandfather and it was hard to concentrate on what he was saying. He kept talking about how expensive everything was, a habit my father and brother had also picked up. His eyes were mine when I was a baby. We were all shuffling around our genes in an attempt to be understood.

The next day the heavy purple curtains were gone. Inside were twelve tables that appeared wooden but looked as though deep down they were plastic. On each table sat a bottle of red sauce and a bottle of brown sauce. The floor was a brisk sheet of linoleum. Behind the tables was a cabinet in which one could see an array of glossy dishes. There were signs that indicated the name of each dish and its price by weight. Everything was clean and translucent. Right from the beginning the Chinese restaurant differentiated itself from the Lebanese restaurant. It did not close between two and seven and between nine and twelve, and on certain Sundays. It did not strive towards complexity. All it did was remain open. Every time I walked past it was open – at 8:30am, at 11:15pm, on Mondays, on Sundays, on Wednesdays, on Christmas Day. I never saw any of its customers. Either they were very discreet or they didn't exist. It seemed that it was not about the customers. Customers were hardly the point. The only point was to stay open.

There were several important people in my life. There was a basic outline, which I filled with different stuffing. There was one role that always had to be filled. It was like one of those movies where as the character gets older the actor keeps getting replaced by someone else; it's the same person, they just look different. It was always a surprise to see who had got the role. It was never the person I expected. It was possibly my imaginary friend Fussa who first occupied the role in my life. I used to draw pictures of her on the wall of my bedroom. The next time I saw her she was a tall, angular man who strode around the streets and played a guitar in some band. I heard someone call him/her RJ once. What could those letters stand for? It was hard for me to look at him without a small convulsion taking place in the bones of my shoulders. He disappeared one day; he was written off in some story about a girlfriend in Tokyo. I waited patiently, trying to fill the vacancy, and eventually he came back in the form of a young woman who wore a waistcoat and worked in a supermarket. I suppose there were certain similarities – the black hair, the height, the weight. This much was consistent. I began making urgent shopping lists. There were sudden late-night cravings for chocolate milk. What was fascinating was that the young woman at the supermarket pre-dated RJ. I'd seen her many times before she had taken up her new role. I looked carefully at apparent strangers, at acquaintances I felt nothing for, studying them for signs of metamorphosis, wondering who would be next. Who *would* be next? The butcher? The next-door neighbour? My good friend's boyfriend? I went away for the summer and when I got back the woman in the supermarket was gone. I felt lost without her. I'd spent the whole month of August trying to think up ways of bringing fiction to life. As with the other times, I was certain that no one else could possibly fill the role and I spent several months in a desperate non-existent space as I roamed around various supermarkets.

Then came the maths teacher who resembled Paul Auster. Again, there was a similar weight range, a similar height. He seemed to know as well as I did who he had become, and looked embarrassed when we ran into each other. There was the curly-haired guy who was a compost expert and helped out at the community garden; he was probably the last person I had expected to take up the role – he was skinnier than the others and he introduced me to a wife and long-haired child one Saturday morning. Then there was that man I'd seen thousands of times before, who wore beige suits and sneakers and sometimes a cape. He too had once been a remote object far off on the horizon. He began to sit closer and closer to me at the café. And then one day he talked. It was amazing to think of how far Fussa had come. She had been this tiny invisible waif and now here she was – a slightly overweight forty-year-old man chain-smoking his way out of the morning.

Once I was in I wanted to get out. I thought fondly of the caterpillar. I met my husband for lunch to talk it over. Public places were good for us. I chose the small, friendly place where people worked on their computers and talking was discouraged. I wanted everyone in the café to hear what I had to say. They would be my witnesses. We sat in the corner and ate ham sandwiches. Because he was my negative, today he was in a light-hearted, trivial mood, although he was disappointed with how much mayonnaise they had put in his sandwich. He thought that mayonnaise was no place for a ham sandwich, and he told me the story about the perfect ham sandwich that his grandfather used to make for him – half a baguette, salted butter, ham and a single thinly sliced gherkin. He'd never mentioned his grandfather before and I encouraged him to go on. Although the bruise on the right side of my jaw was more blue than yellow, we were good friends in many ways.

I might have recently had my wisdom teeth out. The truth was, I had no wisdom teeth at all. The dentist called me a very interesting specimen of evolutionary progress. He was also excited about the baby tooth that was still in my mouth. It was showing no signs of wanting to fall out.

My husband told me that just before his grandfather

died he had left a note saying that he didn't want anyone to come to his funeral. He requested immediate cremation and dispersal. He wanted no one he knew to witness it and he wanted the whole thing to be over with as fast as possible. I said that that was an interesting way of avoiding death. I added that he sounded like a very controlling person. My husband didn't say anything but I could tell by the way he removed the mayonnaise from the corners of his mouth that he did not agree with me. A small Roma boy had come into the café and was going from customer to customer, asking for money. The boy took the time to approach each one personally and ask them for help. He held out his hand and said please. The customers were careful not to make eye contact; they continued typing, releasing only a quick, firm shudder of the head to acknowledge his existence. I admired his persistence. He would not accept anything less than success. I took several gold coins out of my pocket and held them in my hand.

'Listen,' I said, raising my voice so that everyone in the café could hear. I'd said these words so many times but, without listeners, they had the habit of evaporating. 'I'm leaving.'

The present continuous was the recommended tense to use, and I was careful not to use words like 'going to' and 'want to', which indicated desire rather than action, and could be confusing for the auditor. The coins were growing sweaty in my hand, but the boy was now doggedly whittling away at a woman who had made the mistake of looking at him.

'*Ne me quitte pas*,' my husband sang. He went on, imploring me to forget our misunderstandings. He had a good singing voice. It was a song by Jacques Brel, later sung by Nina Simone. Many people in the café turned to listen to his singing and smile at him, at us. They thought it was a wonderful joke. The café owner interrupted the little boy and asked him to leave, and I put the coins back in my pocket.

I heard that it takes at least seven attempts to get out. Seven just happened to be my favourite number. I'd once had a drawn-out relationship with someone who was born on the 7th of the 7th, 1977. At the time it appeared to be fate.

In the meantime, I had other things to do.

I had to go to the supermarket. My mother also used to spend a lot of time at the supermarket. It was a small, sad place full of different versions of oneself which one avoided as best as one could. I tried to keep my eyes down. Things were cheaper down low. I was waiting for someone to create a supermarket where everything was hip-level and below and we could crawl around on our knees like post-Christian believers.

I had gone to great lengths to avoid the supermarket. I had dug up soil from the neighbour's garden and filled tyres and old pots I'd found on the street with it. I'd planted pumpkin seeds and basil, strawberries and mint. I had buried the sprouting potatoes I'd found in the pantry and waited for them to perform. One was shaped like a love-heart and I had hopes that in one hundred days I would dig up a family of love-hearts, even though I knew this was not the way of children.

When I went back in the spring I could not find even the

original love-heart. I used the spade first and then got down on my knees and reached deep into the earth. 'Things don't just disappear!' I said. This was not what we had been taught in sex education.

'Maybe it killed itself,' my son suggested. He delivered this statement as if it were a joke.

I stood in the queue at the checkout and fantasised about taking the person in front of me's groceries home – family packs of mince and bottles of bleach, cans of cassoulet, bottles of orange juice, boxes of *biscottes* and those pots of yoghurt that came seamed together in packs of eight – items that no matter how hard I tried I would never dream of putting in my trolley. Some things you just couldn't do.

There were the black carbon particles that had turned up in the hearts of school children. There was the urban heat island. There were tyres and their tendency to release particles of themselves. There was ubiquitousness and David Attenborough.

There were placentas which, it turned out, could be crossed.

There was that French rock star who didn't mean to kill his girlfriend in an argument. Didn't he once sing a beautiful song about the wind carrying everything away?

There were so many things we'd heard before.

There were also so many other things to do.

There was the pasta to cook (water as salty as the sea) and a salad to make.

'Can't you clean up every now and then?' my husband said. It was old trick we played on each other, an emergency exit, a quick fix. An argument was a good way to prove you cared.

It was a mysterious thing to say to someone who had just spent the morning trying to make the house look like other houses she'd been inadvertently invited into.

Maybe he was referring to the spider webs. The one in the kitchen, erected in the corner between the oven and the fridge so you had to duck every time you wanted a drink, was spectacular. It had been pulled down several times but its maker was efficient in reconstructing it. The location was close to its heart.

It was only later that I realised I had failed to participate in the argument.

There was, I thought, still a chance that I had misread his comment, that he was not flirting with me, but merely asking me a rhetorical question. It could even have been a throwaway remark. People threw away so much these days.

I fell briefly in love with a Kurdish man. He gave definition to the nebulous forms in my head. He articulated the inarticulate. He explained so much to me – about the wondrous age that existed twenty thousand years ago and the Mesolithic and Neolithic societies within the Zagros–Taurus system, when 'no man or woman was the private property of any one person'. I loved hearing stories about this time, about the cultivation of plants, about the hoe and hand-grinder and ox-cart, before the hunter and the hunted. He had a warm smile that sat just under a bushy moustache. Many bad songs have been sung about how he made me feel. He had the strong calloused hands of a baker. He had a big lump of dough that he kept sculpting into meaningful and beautiful things.

He was not a baker. He was one of the founding members of the Kurdish Workers' Party. The Kurdish do not have a state of their own. They belong to four different countries and have no interest in borders. They have struggled for the recognition of their existence.

It was unclear how old Abdullah was. He himself was not sure, blasé about such things as a *date of birth*, but estimated it to be somewhere between 1946 and 1947. I understood that his birth had never been a moment in time;

he was against delineations of any kind. I tried to find out as much as I could about him. He had written several books, one of which was called *Erkeği öldürmek*. There was no English translation. I admired the letters and caressed their decorative accessories with my index finger, trying to be one of those women who could be satisfied with little. In the end I gave in and gave one letter at a time to Google's translator, although by the time I got to the final *k*, I already knew what it meant. That was true love for you. The translator told me that the book was called *Killing the Male*. I might have used other words.

Abdullah is currently in prison on the island of Imrali in Turkey where he has been held in solitary confinement for the last twenty years due to his ideas about achieving peace. It is still unclear whether he is dead or alive. He was sentenced to death on the 29th of June 1999, but before they could kill him Turkey abolished the death penalty. None of his lawyers have been allowed to see him. They have appealed seven hundred times.

The weather forecast that morning was thunderstorms and rain amidst a chaotic sky. I have always surrounded myself with people who talk about the weather.

I thought it was high time someone invented the disinvent movement. I asked my friend Juliette if she thought this was something people could feel excited about. She was working in image consulting and was worried about how it might affect her business.

'Don't worry,' I said. 'It's probably already been invented.'

I got some T-shirts made anyway. *Disinvent Yourself,* it said on them, in fluorescent letters on a black background. I made my children wear them to school and they hated me for it. Their teachers told them 'disinvent' was not a word.

'That's the point,' I told them to tell their teachers.

They replied that they would never tell their teachers anything remotely close to that. They told me they would disinvent my T-shirts.

I'd been the leader of movements before. I'd once set up a car-wash business on our street, then there was the Jesus Club, and the following week the Kool Kids Club. Things moved fast when you were nine. There was no reason why I couldn't do it again thirty years later. So far I had three members. Every week we would disinvent something. This week it would be plastic. Next week it would be the aeroplane. I stood outside the supermarket and handed out flyers, which people kindly refused as they left carrying large packs of bottled water. They shrugged helplessly at me, indicating that their hands were full – otherwise they would gladly have taken one. Plus it was thirty-seven degrees outside. This really wasn't an ideal time for disinvention. Juliette called me to tell me she thought I was going down a slippery slope, that she'd had time to think about it, and, honestly, it was hard to see this was going anywhere.

'Maybe going places is overrated,' I said. 'Look at where going places has got us.'

'What are you going to disinvent next – medicine?'

'Of course not. I was thinking more pharmaceutical companies.'

She proceeded to tell me that pharmaceutical companies supplied a great number of the products that she sold to her clients and had made an enormous difference in their lives. I took the tone in her voice to be a sign of progress, a sign that the Movement was gaining in momentum. Then she put an end to our friendship. 'Who are you,' she said, 'to come along and tell everyone what they should and shouldn't be?'

Who was I?

'You're not acting like yourself,' Juliette told me several weeks later. I never knew how to act like myself. I thought this might mean that I'd successfully disinvented myself, but then she said, 'You're acting like John.'

John was a guy I knew that lived in a caravan. He'd lost most of his teeth and sang pop songs on the side of the road to make a bit of money. When things got rough he gambled on the horses. He wheeled his belongings around in a wheelchair. He'd once been married to a primary-school principal and had two children with her but he'd eventually shed them along with his house and his furniture and his teeth. He used to be a very good-looking guy, someone who knew him told me. He used to be a great lady-killer. It was lucky he didn't get AIDS. My brother used to be a great lady-killer. His name was John, too. Now the ladies are killing him. Juliette thought John was revolting and that he smelled bad. But he could leave whenever he wanted. If John wanted to disinvent a place he just drove away and it was gone.

23

I found several melon flowers growing on the balcony. I didn't know where they'd come from. I had no memory of planting melon seeds. I had to go to the internet to ask for advice. It told me that if I ever wanted a melon it was likely I would have to hand-pollinate, due to the problem of the bees never finding my balcony. Even though they fly, they avoid heights. The female melon flower is only open for one day so you have to work quickly, if possible first thing in the morning between seven and nine. You can either pluck off the male flower directly and rub him up and down on the female or you can take a paintbrush and brush the male stamen and then paint the pollen onto the female. By the end of the day both flowers will have wilted and will eventually fall off. It was not a nice way to read one's own biography and I had to shut the computer for a while and rest before deciding what to do next.

'The Amazon rainforest is on fire,' my husband told me over breakfast.

It always came around so fast. The toast and the coffee, the muesli and the tea. For some reason linked to the free market, today there were kouign-amanns.

Lackadaisical, I read in the dictionary, admiring its floral qualities.

'It's been burning for three weeks,' he said. He wanted me to know that areas the size of fifteen football fields had been burned to smithereens.

It was not a word that was native to his vocabulary. He was always careful to avoid melodrama.

'Into extremely small bits,' I said. 'To complete destruction.'

He told me more things I knew already, about how the rainforest sucked pollution out of the air, how it created moisture that was carried by clouds and released over areas of Brazil otherwise prone to drought. There were already severe cases of drought in São Paulo, which would only be exacerbated, not to mention the vital role the rainforest played in the stability of the biosphere.

This was the way we talked to each other now – through the voices of journalists we'd never met before, through movie reviews and recipe instructions and letters that told us the amount we owed for the temporary use of electricity.

'This is an emergency,' he said.

It was clear that it was my fault.

It was true that I used to order three different beverages at the café.

'What about you?' I said. 'Didn't you used to smoke a pack a day?'

I held out half of my kouign-amann as a peace offering.

'Couldn't we both be complicit?' I said. Didn't we both believe in other people's American dreams? Weren't words like growth, satisfaction and annual yearly profit the words we used to throw around on a weekday? If we didn't use them, we heard them. We breathed them in and we breathed them out again.

'All I'm saying is, you didn't need to buy all those bottles of water,' he said, taking a bite out of the kouign-amann.

I wondered why that had not occurred to me at the time.

I had a few stragglers in the Movement – people who liked to sign petitions and take flyers – mostly the elderly who had time for such extracurricular activities. I don't think the majority of them fully realised what kind of movement they'd signed up for when I convened them to the meetings at the sports bar on the corner – or that they really cared. The question of whether it was Crochet Quarters or Neighbourhood Watch or Christians Anonymous or Anarchy Now was secondary, even irrelevant. The key question was, what time was the meeting? Should they bring a raincoat? Some Louise cake? They went out of their way to run into me at the market on Sunday mornings.

There was Maurice – a twenty-two-year-old unemployed guy who belonged to several semi-professional far left movements and whose passion for the Movement surpassed my own. He had all the ideas, which I typed out on my computer. He thought the first thing to disinvent should definitely be cars. Mavis interrupted him to say that she did use her two-door Toyota to get horse manure for her garden sometimes. There was a brief digression into heirloom tomato varieties. Frank thought it would be better to start small and work our way up. What about kitchen appliances? He hardly ever used the juice squeezer he got three Christmases ago. While I tried to make room for such deliberations, Maurice disregarded them and pressed on with his agenda. People weren't going to disinvent things on their own – they needed us to do that for them. He suggested we begin by painting the windscreens of all the cars in the neighbourhood black between one and three in the morning. Every night we'd attack a new neighbourhood. He liked the image of a man getting in his car to go to work in the morning and finding himself facing a black hole. What could be more poignant than that? Disinvention would be a long process but we must first plant the seed. People would be forced into finding other ways to get to work – although, eventually, we'd disinvent work as well. 'Then, say, a week later,' Maurice went on, 'once people have adjusted to the idea somewhat, we'll throw gasoline over the cars and set fire to them.' Certain members took a break from their good-willed nodding at this point. Hélène voiced a concern about her next-door neighbour Fanny, who was a single mother and had to drop her kids at the childcare place on the other side of town on Tuesdays and Thursdays.

'We'll do it on a Friday,' he said. He already had all the gear – hand-me-downs from another movement. He'd thought about breaking windscreens instead of painting them, which would be more spectacular in a way, but the noise would draw too much attention to the facilitators, and could possibly interrupt the work. Plus, if people really wanted to, they could still drive to work the next morning – all they needed was a bit of plastic, which had not yet been disinvented.

I came home from school one day and kicked in the windscreen of our car. I hadn't expected such a dramatic result. It was just another piece of the universe over which I had no control. And I was only a child. My anger and pain had never made any difference to the outer world. Suddenly I found I was wrong. I was intimately connected to the so-called glass. I watched in horror as my anger fractured into a frightening ten-thousand-piece puzzle I would never be able to put back together again. I think this was the first time I noticed I had a heartbeat.

My mother had always liked European cars that broke down all the time. We regularly went without a car for several months in a row while waiting for the part required to arrive from France. Before the Volkswagen there was the Citroën and before the Citroën there was the Peugeot and before the Peugeot there was Dad. It turned out there had been no progression, as she had been led to believe by the car mechanic. He had all the parts for the Volkswagen but the windscreen was a different matter. Windscreen glass was idiosyncratic stuff. While we waited for our new windscreen to arrive from Germany, we taped up a big piece of plastic that flapped angrily every time we went anywhere. There was a winter trip somewhere when the whole thing came off. It was suddenly quiet – the only sound was the rain hitting the gearbox and the dashboard and the plastic shopping bags piled up in the front seat. Even when the glass came seven months later, car rides and cars felt like humiliating places. Maybe, as Maurice suggested, the screen-breaking was simply the subconscious enactment of my initial idea. He suggested I was just a little ahead of my time.

My mother asked me recently what had provoked such a docile child to do such an aggressive thing – your brother, yes, he would have been capable of kicking in a windscreen, but you, never. It was another case of me not acting like myself. She liked to tell anybody we both knew about how I'd come inside that afternoon and told her that she'd need to take me down to the police station because I was going to jail. She thought it was funny and, sensing this, the people would pretend to laugh.

I told her I did it because she was late to pick me up.

I hated words. They almost always had nothing to do with it.

I tried to bring some more females on board. They were key to the Movement. How had we all just gone along with this whole thing anyway? How had the business model got so out of hand? Why did so many women own one of those tailored jackets? How had nine to five got so holy? Why were we trying so hard to play by the rules? These questions had all been asked and answered before. Hélène gave me a short history lesson on the way home from the sports bar. The thing is, the bra had already been disinvented. It had been disinvented and then it reinvented itself. It rose from the dead. Fire wasn't quite the disinventor we'd all thought it was. Hadn't I heard of the fight for equality? I'd heard of it. That was the problem. She did her best to empathise. She too was unsure about all these ladies wearing nothing but jeans these days – the hoop skirt was once a beautiful thing. I solicited a few random females on the street but they assured me they were very happy. They had no need for a movement in their lives. They had enough on their plates with their jobs and the kids and the housework and the gym. Surely I of all people could understand that.

29

Occasionally I went out to restaurants. There was the Chinese restaurant in Lower Hutt where Dad took us on special occasions. There were wontons and sweet-and-sour pork and spring rolls on a lazy Susan that never stopped turning and the feeling that the world was perfectly round. There was the Korean place on upper Queen Street where Nick told me he was going to Japan because he felt more at home amongst the Japanese. There was the Japanese place on Durham Street where you sat at the counter and ordered small plates of marinated meat. I went there with Dominic when we were pretending to be other people. There was the English place on M.G. Road where I went with Pradeep, who was trying to comfort me with English food even though the food tasted like it was homesick for India. I never did understand what a non-veg cutlet was. There was that expensive place I went to with Dad, where he touched on the horror of being himself. There was that tiny Bangladeshi place on Great North Road that looked like a doctor's waiting room where they made perfect dal palak. There was Prego on Ponsonby Road where my mother's girlfriend took us and we were allowed to order whatever we wanted. There was that place in Florence where Juliette and I went and sat talking with two Italians, sustaining a three-hour conversation even though nobody spoke each other's language. There was the Italian pizzeria in Paris where the owner would come around and tell people who were outstaying their welcome that it was time to leave. There was that place in Dunedin which strictly speaking was not a restaurant, where I watched my sister pick the blueberries out of the muffin she'd been ordering every day for breakfast for the last twenty years. It seemed she was not interested in the rest.

Each morning I knew I was closer to leaving. This was not so much about walking out the door as it was dismantling a whole system of belief. I thought about the cheap drawers we'd bought at Ikea which we'd spent all afternoon and evening assembling, the pale planks of wood and different-sized screws lying in the middle of the floor. The guy in the shop had told us it would take fifteen minutes. It was clear by 1am that he had no experience in relationships.

Now it was just a matter of getting down on the floor and undoing all those screws. It required concentration and a methodical approach, neither of which the modern world had equipped me with. I had an infantile longing for a manual, for an alphabetical order. I had once formed part of a team that helped write those manuals. We had been instructed not to use numbers but letters in the step-by-step process. The alphabet had a sense of mortality that numbers did not, which was ultimately reassuring to the consumer.

We had been one of those couples that walked around the make-believe kitchens and bedrooms and bathrooms of the Ikea warehouse, thinking that the sum of all those kits we bought would be a place like this. That we too would have a kitchen with pots hanging on hooks, a bright yet sober bedroom with creaseless clothes in the wardrobe and pairs of shoes that fit into the designated shelves. We bought the hooks for the pots but never got around to putting them up. The pieces of furniture we had assembled sat around, refusing to knit together. I often sat around drinking tea on them, wondering what had gone wrong.

My musician friend was worried because he was running out of money. I often met him at the place on Rue Robespierre, which was an expensive restaurant except in the mornings, when it was still a cheap café.

'I'm doing exactly the same thing I've always done,' he said, 'but it's not working anymore.'

He'd always busked on the street and made at least one or two hundred euros a day.

'If things keep going like this I won't be able to pay my rent.'

He sipped his coffee.

'I'm not worried,' he added.

I asked him why he didn't just change a small thing: the guitar he used, or the places he busked.

'Why would I change what I've always done?'

He changed the subject to his girlfriend, which was another problem he had. He liked her a lot, but things had to be a certain way. He was only allowed to see her once a week, on particular days, and now he was not sure he was ever going to see her again. He'd tried calling her up to see if she would like to meet him for a drink and she'd hung up on him.

'I think I'm afraid of her.'

She sounded like the kind of person we needed more of in the Movement and I asked him for her number.

'So anyway,' he said. 'How are you?'

I never knew how to answer that question.

There was a sense of dictatorship in the air. It bore a resemblance to freedom. We had no idea who the dictator was but I had recently noticed that silence had its own kind of noise. Sometimes there were thousands of birds just out of hearing's reach.

I wondered if the dictator was not the woman with the short, blonde haircut who had interviewed me for a job. It wasn't just that her name rhymed with Mussolini. There was a large energy field around her and she resembled a Francis Bacon painting, exposing terrifying angles of herself.

As she explained the role in more detail and the person I would be replacing (incompetent, uninspired, ill-equipped), I wondered if the fascist was not so much in her as in the low ceilings, the architecture of her office, possibly even in the freedom she had to quickly check something online. She mentioned once again the excellent Wi-Fi throughout the building.

She was a powerful artist and I could feel how close I was to becoming another of her sharp angles. After all, I needed the money. She wondered if I might like to join the team right then and there. I had to concentrate to keep my eyes fixed on her blind spot until I was safely out of the building.

33

I liked that Italian guy who had got to the bottom of the French language. He'd made an enormous Caprese salad that sat on the table dominating the room. We kept helping ourselves to it but it made no difference.

'France is the only country in the world where the majority of its people can't write their own language properly. It is specifically designed to keep people out. It keeps the elite feeling elite and everyone else feeling like a piece of shit.'

Then he gave a long speech about the superiority of the Italian language, which I paid no attention to. I was looking at the amazing view of the ugly side of Paris out the window.

We tried to convince him to come to a party with us but he was unconvinced. We drank another bottle of wine and tried again. He turned to the two males to his left and said, 'Listen, how about you take all your clothes off and then I'll come to the party.'

Later, I regurgitated his arguments to two professors in a high-ceilinged room.

They dismissed his claims with a few spare words.

34

The woman who resembled my mother came to pick us up and take us to the party. Just like my mother, she said she'd be there at nine thirty. She'd said she was just leaving work and would be there in fifteen minutes. For a few minutes I believed her. I wished things could be different.

When she turned up at ten fifty-six with a string of white lies, I turned away from them and nodded mildly out the window, looking for Mercury in the night sky, which I'd heard would be visible for several days while the earth was on its axis, although maximum visibility was during the twilight hours, which were now long gone.

This was what it was to be an adult. To forgive and forget. To sleep in the bed that you made. To cut the coat to suit the cloth. To be mutton dressed up as lamb. It was true that she was wearing tights made out of a fabric I worried was imitating leather.

'Maybe I won't come after all. I'm feeling a bit had it.' I yawned to illustrate the extent of my fatigue.

'Don't throw a tantrum,' she said and told me to get in the car.

I went straight to the dance floor and tried to burn off some anger. The party wasn't how I had imagined it. Something about the helium balloons and the cucumber sandwiches. The way everyone seemed to be having a good time. The woman who resembled my mother came up to me and handed me a samosa in a serviette.

'You must be starving,' she said.

I thought I was going to end up kissing the guy with the greasy hair and the distinctive dance style on the couch in the corner. But things didn't happen like they used to. Instead I left with another mature woman I had met in the toilets. She had a bottle of champagne with her and had just finished drawing a straight line of black ink across her eyelids. I admired those women who took the time to remake themselves. I was just washing my hands with pink soap, but she asked me if I wanted to go see this band that was playing at the Purgatory. It was a covers band that kind of sucked but anything had to be better than this shitty party.

Outside the stars were burning up in a pale sky. I thought I recognised Mars somewhere out there. It took us forty-five minutes to get to the Purgatory which was, like the party, not as I had imagined it. Through the dirty windows we could see that the band had finished playing, its members sitting around in light that brought out their hopes and dreams. We'd come all this way now, though. We were freezing and tired. There was nothing else to do but go in.

On my birthday, I was taken to a hotel that had once been a prison. It had been renovated in such a way as to preserve its particularities, with passionfruit flowers and other creepers entwined around the bars over the windows. An absence of a television, telephone, fridge and kettle. The double bed that lay stripped in the middle of the room looked more like a single. Instead of a bathroom there was a velvet curtain, hung somewhere between poverty and decadence. With the view of the sea, the tinted bottles of shampoo, conditioner and body wash, and the notepad on the desk that said *I woke up feeling inspired*, it was less a hotel and more an example of prison reform.

It was the doors to the rooms that had absorbed most of the history. The numbers stamped on them had the bare font of prisoners. Like bodies, they were heavy and took two people to move.

My husband was eager to get out and explore the landscape. I preferred the hallways, which veered in unpredictable directions and led to rooms and alcoves unwilling to be identified. We spent some time in one, trying to give it a name. There was a wooden ladder that reminded me of our relationship. It was attached to a concrete wall and led up to the ceiling. The room would not be defeated by us and in the end we left it unbaptised. We went back to our room for a meal. I thought they would have room service, that it would be part of the hotel's philosophy, but I was informed that this also belonged to the world they were trying to protect their guests from.

There wasn't much else to do but go out.

The number of artists at the art gallery was overwhelming. It seemed there were too many. There were too many. Never would so many poems be assembled in a single building and people expected to walk around and read each one. It seemed an unfair burden that had been placed on the visitors, but that is exactly what they were determined to do. I could not stop crossing paths with one woman in particular. I was walking across the room to look at some bright colours; she was going the other way in search of geometric shapes. I took a last-minute left into musicalism; she was lingering between two violins. I took a right into a hallway ill-advised to those prone to epilepsy, but she got there before me. She was doing her best to get away from me as well, judging from her lips, which grew increasingly thin as we both made abrupt diagonal lines in opposite directions. But the art was stronger than us and persisted in pushing us together in nonsensical arrangements. I was always running into the people I least wanted to see. In the end I left the art gallery to get away from her. I sat outside in the grey sun, exhausted, blinded by art, unable to recall a single painting. All I could see was that unremarkable woman in her white T-shirt, her black hair parted severely down the middle, her sensible sneakers that were white and black.

'This is about freedom,' he said when we got back from the art gallery.

I was drinking black coffee and reading the dictionary again, a habit of his and an experiment of mine.

Abeyance it said. *Let's hold that problem in abeyance for a while.*

I nodded vaguely in the style of someone busy with the internet, even if it was a large, heavy, physical book with 1229 pages and the cover torn off. It was so huge and physical that it was making me feel sweaty and light-headed, although this may have been the coffee. How could so many words exist? Why choose one over another? Faced with this vast ecosystem that lived, supposedly, in my own head, words great and small crawling around, dozing, incubating, I had to take another sip of coffee.

He asked me what I thought, and when I didn't reply, he asked me what I was thinking. I told him I was thinking about my grandfather. This was not altogether a lie. Alzheimer's had killed off a large part of his ecosystem. Every now and then he'd come out with a rare species. Last time I'd seen him he'd leant forward in his soft beige armchair of which many replicas had been arranged in social configurations around the rest home and said, 'Isn't this the wilderness?' He seemed a bit emotional, as if he knew it would be the last time he would use that word. I wondered if pathological forgetfulness was what had happened to the earth. My husband wanted to know what my grandfather had to do with our relationship.

I glanced down at the dictionary, letting my eyes fall on whichever word would help me. There was something soothing about *and*. It was a word you could rely on. I liked it immensely.

38

I woke up to the usual thirty-second panic. I was more at home asleep. It was a chance to see all the people I hadn't seen for years, do things, go places. Here there was a multicoloured duvet cover that was clearly a mistake and a ceiling dotted with the bloody remains of old mosquitos. A woman was talking to her dog on the street outside.

'What are you doing?' she said. 'Come on, what in Christ's name are you doing?'

An oppressive silence emanated from below. How could I have ended up in a place like this? Out the window were different-coloured oblong shapes that an artist might have been able to turn into something meaningful. I was born in a bland house by the sea. My mother didn't like it there. There were squashed mosquitos on the ceiling and the linen was the wrong colour. And my father kept knocking her unconscious. I had always admired her for getting out. The next time I saw her I got out my notebook and asked her how she did it.

'Very slowly,' she said.

39

There was just that Renoir & Friends exhibition that was in its last days. It had been on for six months but now I realised how urgent it was that I go. I wasn't an enormous fan of Renoir but I was interested in meeting his friends. There were rumours going around that he was a misogynist cunt, which had been an effective marketing technique.

In order to meet Renoir's friends, however, you were obliged to meet Renoir first. I tried to walk in the back way, but a security guard escorted me back to Renoir where all the other females were.

I increased my pace, admiring how clean and white the walls were, which reminded me of another exhibition I'd been to – a gothic fresco that I had to go back and see the following week. It was that sort of love. It turned out to be unrequited; the wall where the fresco had been was now the devastating shade of white that is only ever seen in art galleries. I feigned the casual register of the out-of-love and asked the attendant about it. He told me that the artist wasn't happy with his work and had decided to paint over it. It was vaguely comforting that it was still there somewhere, and I went back several more times to look at the fresco concealed under three layers of paint.

40

'Would you rather,' Juliette said, 'have tea with the Queen in a hot-air balloon or coffee with the French president in a submarine?'

She only asked me this because we had run out of things to say. I was running out of a lot at the moment. I'd run out of both milk and bread that morning. I knew what she was getting at though.

Good bread or good times. Polite folk who asked you how you were or honest dudes that didn't give a fuck. A clear sky with a clean wind or the smoggy comfort of the Mediterranean. A glass or a mug. Cinnamon or chocolate.

I asked her if there was any way I could have tea with the Queen in a submarine.

She was afraid not.

She sipped her coffee, which left its residue in the cracks of her dry lips.

'Would you rather have sex without a condom with the guy you're crazy about or accept cunnilingus from a guy that's crazy about you?'

This turned out to be an actual problem she had.

'Go for the cunnilingus.'

'But I really like him.' She knocked over her coffee to show me how much she liked him and there were a few moments when we both enjoyed the distraction of black coffee being absorbed by a cream serviette.

41

The children went away for a while and were replaced by a thirty-something unshaven man. There was something of Abdullah in his moustache. He was a friend of Maurice's and needed a place to stay for a few days. My husband and I took him for a walk by the river and pointed out the motorboats and the flying fox. We bought him an ice cream. We went home via the bookshop and made him lunch. We asked him too many questions about what he wanted to do tomorrow. He became moody and silent and sculpted valleys of couscous on one side of his plate. I asked him if he had something against couscous and he said not particularly. He liked to sit upstairs on the balcony and look at the basil. We had never had so little to say to one another. I began hoping that Maurice's friend would go away. Our relationship was unravelling under the enormous strain of a witness. I had never noticed how sad and lonely we were before. Aside from the violence, there were moments when we appeared to be in love. We went outside into the garden to get away from him, but he followed us out there. We went back upstairs into the kitchen but he too wanted refreshments. We went out to the movies but even when he wasn't there we found we couldn't get away from him anymore. I'd read stories about those people who come into your house and pull the couches away from the wall and shine torches into the corners and empty all your clothes out onto the floor and push the bed over onto the other side of the room so you can finally see the filth you have been living in. I think there were television shows about them. They just turned up at your house one day and gave you a fright.

42

Maurice's friend was the one who pointed out the plum tree in the neighbours' garden and the branch that hung provocatively over our fence. We admired it out the dirty living-room window, letting it buoy our conversation for a few minutes as we sipped weak tea. We considered the foggy mauve of the plums and whether this was the shade that signified ripeness. Right now the plums were all we had in common and we were thorough in exhausting the subject. Maurice's friend's aunt in Devon had a plum tree he used to climb up, but they were damson plums – a rounder shape, a redder colour. His aunt used to make him sit in the back garden and take all the stones out of them. She'd given him fifty pence for every hundred stones. I told him about my own childhood plum tree that produced only three or four plums a year that were always bitter and yellow. We went through the varieties, the colours, the seasons. We both recognised it as the potential exit route out of our strangerliness but neither of us were ready to say anything. I opened the window to break the silence that had crystallised between us as we lingered near the tree, waiting for it to nourish us with more words. A fat pigeon settled on one of the branches and flapped its wings, and the branch swung violently as it adjusted once again to lightness. There was a dull thud in the next-door garden.

43

There was the brief exhilaration of thirty plums in a bucket on a glary Sunday morning, but the expression on Maurice's friend's face (pride, frustration, unrest) told me this was not the end. He gave me a detailed description of the oozing blanket of waste all over the grass next door, which his trip up the ladder had allowed him to witness. He described once more the branches that were unbearably burdened by their own weight. Words like 'jam' and 'Christmas presents' were evoked as well as the taste of a plum in winter. There were three more thuds, closely spaced together.

I stood on the fourth rung of the ladder and held the bucket while he threw the plums over from the other side. If there were any signs of neighbourhood watch, I was to descend the ladder, hide the bucket in the bush of stinging nettle, and call out, 'Have you found it?'

I had never felt so close to someone.

44

We were happy for about forty-five minutes. There were bowls of plums all over the house and we wandered around in blank euphoria, as rosy as they were. By five o'clock Maurice's friend had grown fidgety and I was beginning to get anxious about what we were going to do with all of them. He abruptly told me he was going out to get some beer. I began destoning the plums in the kitchen. I had no idea how to make jam but there were no excuses anymore with the internet. Maurice's friend still wasn't back at ten. I'd made one dubious batch of jam and filled all the cereal bowls with it because I didn't have enough jars. The house was pungent with plumness and I hadn't even got through a third of them. The weight of them grew too much for me and I had to go to bed. I didn't see Maurice's friend until the morning he left. It was unclear if he was avoiding me or if he just happened to always be asleep. It was true that he had the habit of mostly sleeping in the day. I tried to give him jars of jam to take with him when he left, but he refused, saying that he wasn't such a big fan of plum jam.

45

The Movement lagged after Maurice's friend left. Maurice was preoccupied with dispersing the apathy that had settled into the heart of the Anarchist Party. He told me that it was important to do something about it before it solidified into something more threatening, like heart disease. I was in some kind of listless awe after Maurice's friend's reckless departure. Could men leave in a way that women couldn't?

Before, if you wanted to get out you just jumped in the car and drove up north. 'Jumping in the car' was still something that you could do. I didn't like the way Maurice's friend had 'jumped in the car'. I loved it and I hated it. You might stop at a roadside café for a cup of tea and an over-iced piece of carrot cake. You might jot down a few paragraphs about your feelings since you'd left and the events that had prompted you to jump in the car in the first place. You might describe the 'naked coastline' and the 'tide pulling at the blood in your brain'. You might strike up a conversation with the person in the café who asked you for a light and hear about his feelings about things as well, along with his descriptions of the landscape. Before, it was your story – about what you wanted and the way to go about it. Now it had nothing to do with you. Jumping in the car was a loaded exercise. You might think you were making the story your own. You might think you were going somewhere, but the only place you were going was far into your own feelings. What did your feelings have to do with it? Insects were dying. It was preposterous to say things like 'he thought' and 'she felt'. That morning I had read in the newspaper that hover flies were dying, and that the event heralded the collapse of everything. Further down the page there was an extract from the last remaining letter found on the *Titanic*, which mentioned the lovely weather and excellent food on board. The letter had just sold for 135,000 pounds.

46

I wanted to get out. Sometimes getting out required another angle in. I needed to be more like my brother. I drew a diagram. The diagram told me that the main obstacle to getting out was money. Money was like God, something you tried your best not to believe in, until you realised how much you needed it. That's why I'd applied for the position in the first place.

The office was further away than I'd anticipated and there were several moments during the journey when I contemplated turning back. It looked easy to just get off. Other people did it. And there was a drinks machine right there, where you could put a coin in and experience the undeniable pleasure of carbonated water. I too was a consumer with a short attention span. I too was a girl who just wanted to have fun.

It was clear, however, that I wasn't going anywhere.

God was keeping a close eye on me. After the train there was a bus that didn't come. We all stood at the bus stop in the spitty rain and looked for it. It occurred to me that I would be late.

When the bus finally came there were about one hundred and twenty of us. I wanted to hang back and play hard to get like in the old days, assert my independence and wait for the next bus. But I pushed and shoved like the rest of them.

Bus 113 suddenly meant as much to me as it did to them.

I watched the landscape change from respectable-looking buildings with well-groomed geraniums in the windows to semi-detached blocks of grey, then to vast stretches of buildings that I was afraid people lived in, each one a poorer imitation of the one before. The colour of these buildings no longer resembled anything as bright as grey but had deteriorated into another more ambivalent colour that did not yet have a name. It seemed an unlikely place to earn a bit of cash and I double-checked with the bus driver that this was the right stop.

47

As I pressed the buzzer of the building, I still hoped that I would be able to make it back to the bus before the bus driver finished his cigarette and turned the whole operation in the other direction.

My hopes were promptly destroyed as the door opened and I was escorted through several hallways and introduced to my future colleagues. I could tell from the way they smiled at me that they were a little embarrassed to see me here too. I learned during the coffee break that one was a sculptor; he made tiny figurines he likened to poems. Another was interested in sound vibrations. An older woman identified strongly with astrology. They hadn't been expecting to wash up in this yellow kitchen either, sharing two tea-bags between four. We were a small congregation.

They were kind, though, and showed me where the toilets and the photocopy machine were. These were also things, along with money, that I might need. They reassured me that although it took a long time to get there, time went by quickly.

'It's a bit like Narnia, you know,' the sculptor said. 'It feels like ages when you're here but you get home and it's like only five minutes have gone by in the grand scheme of things.'

I wondered which grand scheme he was referring to. He was onto something, though. His job was just a make-believe fairyland ruled over by a dictator. His grand scheme was elsewhere.

48

Instead of the supposed maturing effect, jobs always took me back to childhood. I found myself once again in neutral-coloured hallways with people I thought I had left behind in Waiwhetū. They looked completely unlike themselves and spoke a different language, but I could tell it was them from the way they addressed me from a great professional height. I was inclined to take a left into the toilets when I saw them coming. I woke up in the morning with the exact same scrunched-up ball of metal in my intestines – it was one of those golden stainless-steel pads we'd used for getting the scrambled eggs off the bottom of the pot. Juliette told me this was just a sign that it was the wrong job. The right job was supposed to make you feel like the powerful owner of your life, such as the job that she had. I found jobs had a way of obscuring their actual purpose, which got confusing. When my first contract ended, I had, in theory, perhaps not enough money to jump in my own car but enough to jump in someone else's. Instead of doing this, I signed another contract. They pushed a piece of paper across the desk and unclicked a pen, and I made an illegible scribble they assumed was my name.

49

I ran into my husband in the kitchen a few days later. I wouldn't have been there at all if it hadn't been for the piece of toast that had got stuck in the toaster.

'Did you know that's extremely dangerous?' he said. He was one of those people who thought that a wooden spoon was the only way to get a piece of toast out of the toaster.

'Some people believe that.'

'That says so much about you.'

I took note of the register, which was flat rather than interested. This was what had first drawn me to him – the unusual blandness of his declarations. 'I love you,' he'd once said to me with a tone of regret and matter-of-factness.

'It's not all about beliefs, you know,' he added.

'Hold on.' I'd managed to get the piece of toast halfway out of the toaster but the uneven crust had got ensnared between two metal bars and I needed my full concentration to get it out without sabotaging the whole operation. I'd always enjoyed using tweezers to remove the tiny organs from the body.

'I can't watch.' A fact rather than an emotion.

I was now using a serrated knife to guide the whole slice up the toaster on a ninety-degree angle.

I heard the newspaper being picked up, its pages turned

in swift succession. I wanted to tell him that it was an old newspaper. I'd just got it out to wrap the glass I'd broken – the scene that had come just before the toast – but I couldn't, with all the concentration it was taking not to electrocute myself.

'Fates of humans and insects intertwined.'

I wasn't so keen on people reading the headlines out loud, but I didn't mind it that morning. It felt like the right thing to say right then, even if it was old news.

50

I had an affair. It could have been with anyone but it was with Maurice's friend. We were in the middle of a Disinvent meeting and Maurice's phone rang. It was winter and actual snowflakes were falling out of the sky. Hélène was concerned that they were too perfect. We listened as Maurice guided the person he was talking to through the geographical whereabouts of a key that had been hidden under a rhododendron pot. The person clearly didn't know what a rhododendron looked like. Maurice then reached over and handed the phone to me.

'It's for you,' he said.

I didn't say hello. I held the phone to my ear and listened to the person exhaling tobacco smoke. I watched as the snow merged back into rain.

'It's me,' the person finally said.

I liked the way he said that, as if he didn't need a name. That must have been the high point in our relationship.

We met at the swimming pool two mornings a week. We did lengths in adjacent lanes and had sex in a cubicle afterwards. The first time, I didn't recognise him in the swimming cap and the tight lycra underpants that were obligatory for males in French swimming pools. He had to come up to me and introduce himself. But I grew to recognise his muscles and the mole the shape of a comma on the left-hand side of his back. I remembered the doctor's advice and kept my jandals on.

It was good to strip back to our swimsuits. Sometimes we had mint tea at the Moroccan place afterwards, but we often ended up arguing. He liked to talk about dead poets and his jaw stiffened when I asked him questions about himself. We got on better without our clothes on.

Occasionally we went back to his one-room place. I didn't understand why he had needed a place to stay when clearly he had a place of his own. He was reluctant to answer the question when I asked him. He had an aversion to rationality. While he played the ukulele, I tried to build up my knowledge of him from the few clues he left hanging around. Piles of books were used as small tables, with coffee cups and ashtrays cluttered on them. I moved a cup and picked a book off the top of a pile and read the author's biographical note. She was Hungarian and had always written in French.

There was a street sign in the corner of the room that had been physically removed from a street in Paris. *Passage Walter Benjamin*, it said.

'Do you like his work?' I asked.

He shrugged, unable to make a commitment either way.

I deduced a weakness for public property. He turned up at my place one day carrying a fire hydrant. It was a dangerous time to come, just before I was due to pick up the kids from school, but I could see straight away that he had the clear-sighted determination of the drunk.

I thought I was onto something when I found hanging in the toilet a framed black-and-white photograph of a woman – I could see the resemblance in the wide-set eyes. When I asked him whether it was his grandmother or great-grandmother perhaps, he told me that he'd found the portrait in a second-hand shop. He'd liked the mercurial expression on her face. That's what he liked about me too, he said.

51

There was nothing quite like a secret. I hadn't had one since I was eight and a half and I'd forgotten how exhilarating it was – and how quickly it morphed into an unbearable burden. I'd only lasted a day before I'd told Jeremy Quinn that Abigail Spinks was in love with him. In this case, however, even the secret had become a secret from itself. As long as it was untold it could still be untrue. The only proof of its existence was the e-ticket that I kept in a folder in a folder in a folder called Untitled, which I kept in a place called Trash. It lived in some realm akin to Lethe, waiting for someone to take the trash out. I liked having the secret in this place where it was both true and false, alive but not altogether so. I avoided the folder for several days, and even when I took a peek it was hard to believe it had anything to do with me. The internet itself had been surprised by my actions and had asked me several times if I was sure that I wanted to go ahead with the purchase. Pop-up ads kept appearing, exposing half-price Italian leather sandals and Armani handbags and silk shirts in the colours of jellyfish. The ads made me think of my father, who was averse to whimsical trips and always encouraged me to spend my pocket money at the mall.

The secret was safe in the trash, where there was no risk that I would share it – although I got close that evening with the sculptor, after the work meeting gave way to several straight shots of vodka on ice. I leant back to look at the stars, which the vodka had been good to, while he admired my neck. Necks were his weakness, he said, when it came to sculpting. I don't think he meant to kiss it, and he apologised immediately afterwards. 'Sorry' was also one of my husband's favourite words. The vodka had a strong undertow. It was pulling me down towards the contents of the trash basket. It reminded me of the beach at Paraparaumu, and there was a brief throb of the nausea associated with homesickness.

52

It was hard to break up with someone with whom you were not even in a relationship. I attempted it anyway. Things could not go on like this.

'Things cannot go on like this,' I said.

Maurice's friend was making tea in the kitchen – a drawn-out process that we usually built our conversations around. He laughed at the tone of melodrama I had introduced into the afternoon.

'Hold on – do you want a biscuit? I found these wonderful biscuits at Xavier's.'

Xavier was both a friend and a shop. Just as I was both a stranger and a lover, a friend and a cocksucker. With him, people were always both, never one or the other. Even though he liked to chat to me for hours about P.G. Wodehouse and the quality of his humour, he also liked to push my head in the direction of his penis. He was always trying to be in several places at once. It was unclear if he lived in Paris, France or Hamburg, Germany; if he was an IT consultant or a co-partner in his friend's wine business; if he was reading Krishnamurti or Rimbaud. He brought out two cups of tea and a plate of the famous biscuits. I took one. It was covered in sesame seeds and tasted of cardamom. It was sweet but not altogether unsavoury.

'What were you saying?'

I told him again, rearranging the words slightly, determined not to be distracted by the biscuits. He thought for a minute, refraining from both tea and biscuits.

'Why can't they?'

It was hard to think of a reason. There was an intense merging of birds and traffic outside – it was rush hour.

'Could they?' he said.

'I don't think so.'

He dipped a biscuit in his tea and ate it, and considered the person sitting on the floor of his living room. How had I got there?

'It would be nice if they could,' he said after a while.

It had grown dark in the room but neither of us got up to turn the light on. It was exactly like the dream I'd had the previous night. I kept walking into rooms that were very dark, and wondered out loud why no one turned the light on.

He tried to protest without actually protesting. 'It's just that I've gotten sort of used to you,' he said eventually.

'I've gotten used to you too,' I said.

We stopped seeing each other not long after that, and I finally got around to emptying the trash basket.

53

Maurice came to see me one Friday night in October. In an age of phones, it was alarming to hear a knock on the door and it took me a few seconds to pull myself together and open it.

'You look like shit,' he said.

I asked him if he'd like a cup of tea. Since I'd had a job this was the sort of thing I asked people. He put down the two big plastic bags and the can of black paint he was carrying and sat on my corduroy couch. I made chamomile tea while he elaborated.

'You look like a big hunk of clay that's had someone's hands all over you like they thought you might make a nice salad bowl.'

'How are you, Maurice?'

He told me he'd recently broken up with his girlfriend. She'd been reading his texts and spying on him in various other ways, and then the whole thing came to a head and she threw his phone in the river.

'Best thing she's ever done for me.'

He dipped the coconut biscuit I had put on the saucer into his tea and sort of sucked it.

'Now, I don't have to worry about anyone tracing my messages. Much safer this way.'

The black eyeliner was smudged on his left eye and I had to quell my maternal urge to lick my little finger and wipe under his eye.

'Anyway, I've got the stuff.'

He took several slurps of tea.

'What stuff?'

'*The stuff.*'

He glared at the plastic bags he'd dropped by the table.

'We need to get this on the road.'

It took me a while to work out what he was talking about.

'What – tonight?'

'Yep. It's better if we don't fuck around with planning – it only creates more opportunities for interference.'

I yawned.

'Listen, Maurice, I've been at work all week. I'm kind of exhausted.'

He got up and started taking rollers and brushes out of the bags.

'You're lucky I know that's not you talking.'

I protested some more but he forged on with what he was doing, wedging the tip of his pocket-knife under the paint lid to prise it open, ignoring me in a way that came across as professional. I guess he'd been through a lot of cold feet before.

'What about the others?'

'I'm sure they won't mind. Have you got a stick or something I can stir this with?'

I rummaged around in the drawers.

I handed him the single chopstick I'd found and told him I was going to get dressed.

'Don't do that,' he said, stirring.

He told me it was best to blend into the night. That way if we ran into anyone I could play at putting out the rubbish.

'I should have worn my pyjamas too.'

I went and put on some socks anyway, and brushed my teeth. But when I came out of the bathroom, Maurice asked me if I had a movie or something we could watch while we were waiting.

'I thought we were doing it now?'

'I think it's best we wait till at least one forty-five.'

I tried to bargain him down to midnight, but he got that hardened bureaucratic look on his face again and told me that 2am was statistically the time that most people were asleep and that the only way he was going to do this was properly.

'I can't let what happened to the Party happen to the Movement,' he said.

I made some coffee and we watched Hitchcock's *Notorious*, which was the only movie I ever watched. Maurice had never seen it before. He remained calm and quiet throughout, except at the end when Devlin and Alicia are walking down the stairs with Alex and his mother. At that point I felt him edging forward on the couch and his breathing became laboured.

On our way out the door, I remembered the real reason I couldn't go.

'The kids – they're asleep upstairs.'

My children were so much a part of me that I sometimes

forgot they were separate beings of their own. Aside from the sheen that had developed over his eyes over the last two hours, Maurice's face remained immune to my excuses.

'They'll be fine. We'll be just around the corner.'

54

The first car was the hardest. It was my neighbour's car – a red BMW that he spent every Saturday morning polishing with this special yellow cloth he'd bought online. Under the debilitating weight of paranoia, it took me about seven minutes to paint the whole windscreen, not helped by the presence of my neighbour's ginger cat, who watched the entire operation with large yellow eyes. Maurice had done three windscreens in the time it took me to do one and, although one of the rules was that we didn't talk to each other during the operation, he gave me a good sharp glare that told me I was behind schedule. After Johnny's car, however, a serene momentum buoyed my movements. That first car had been the moment you dive into the freezing lake, and thereafter was gorgeous weightlessness. As I looked back up the street at the line of black windscreens, the sight of our achievements filled me with elation. Was this what Juliette was talking about? This was as close as I had got to feeling like the owner of my life – whatever the hell that meant. We'd got through three streets and a car park and I'd been back to check the kids once without encountering a single middle-of-the-night drunk. The black sky – there was not even a moon – felt like it was blessing us as we spread its colour across the earth. Maurice was still slightly ahead of me and was already onto street number four when the dazzling black silence was broken by the sound of sirens. I was halfway through the windscreen of a white SUV. Maurice was too far ahead for me to consult with him about whether I should finish or not. In a way, half a windscreen was more conspicuous than a whole. I spent about a quarter of a second trying to assess whether the sirens were getting closer or further away, but it was like trying to work out which way the wind was blowing on a still day. So I proceeded with the emergency plan we'd discussed beforehand and edged under the SUV with my bucket of paint.

55

There was more than one set of sirens. I tried to visualise my children walking downstairs in the morning and fixing themselves bowls of cornflakes. I could see them pouring the milk and sprinkling on too much sugar. I could see them spooning mouthfuls in and drinking the milk out of the bowls. I tried to visualise further but the scene stopped there. There were only more spoonfuls of cornflakes. I comforted myself that my husband would eventually return from his work trip to London and put an end to breakfast. The sirens got closer. At some point I realised the closeness was not as close as it had once been and then it was not close at all. I don't know how long I stayed under the SUV. There had been no sirens for some time, but I was waiting for the silence that had come before to come again. There were many disconcerting noises that there had not been before. Window shutters banged, aeroplanes flew, cats meowed. The sirens had pierced a hole in the silence and let everything through. Maybe an hour went by, maybe ten minutes. I left my paint can under the car and went to look for Maurice. I whispered his name into the night and looked under all the cars on the adjacent street but, like God, he never answered.

It was best I went away for a while. I'd woken up with some strain of hangover I'd never had before. I staggered into the kitchen looking for the extra-strong tablets that combined three drugs, which I kept for special occasions. The children were sitting at the kitchen table eating cornflakes just as I had imagined them.

'Take it easy on the sugar,' I think I said.

They wanted to know why there was black paint on my hands.

'I'm an artist,' I told them.

They wanted to see my paintings.

'They're not finished yet,' I said, and there was a painful jab in my stomach as I remembered the windscreen I'd left half-done three streets away.

It was quiet outside. I didn't like the quiet. Saturday morning was usually all chit-chat and babies. I had expected at least a bit of outrage. The brooding silence was attacking my imagination in a way I hadn't prepared for. This, along with the realisation that the minute we walked out the door the children would see my paintings, led me into the toilet. I needed to think.

We ran into my neighbour on the way to the train station. He was coming back from the supermarket with a bottle of white spirit and a pack of toilet paper. I kept my hands behind my back and my eyes on the children while he told me what I already knew. I said *Oh my God* several times in the spaces he left for this purpose. We'd done a messier job than I'd thought – there were drops of black paint over several car doors. It looked like there had been a bit of rain as well, which had made some of the paint run in grey streaks down several hoods.

'The police are on their way over,' he said.

I told him we'd better get going as we had a train to catch.

'Did they get you too, did they? Bloody hooligans.' He shook his head just like my father did when words failed him.

'We don't have a car,' one of the children told him.

'They're bad for the environment,' another one added.

I'd taken my eyes off them for a second.

In Switzerland everyone was close to nature. Only several large banking corporations stood between them and the mountains. It was expensive but at least it was neutral. I smuggled the children into the single hotel room (twin beds) and went out to look for food. There was nothing on our street except banks and shops that sold watches. I persevered, walking through a big green park and up a hill. There were expensive restaurants and a striking mosaic drawing of Mercury – the closer you got to it the less you could see. Mercury was only Mercury from a distance. Up close he was just tiny pieces of rock. I walked down the other side of the hill into a street called *rue de l'enfer*. I turned the corner and came across a square full of people eating wide bowls of saffron-coloured pasta ribbons. There was a street full of overbearing foodless shops and intricate lettering. I wondered how long I had left the children alone and had a moment of regret that I had not left them in charge of the remote control. I finally returned with three packets of potato chips, a bunch of bananas and a box of muesli. They had already located and mastered the remote control. I spread out my single white towel on the floor and we made a picnic.

'It's nice here,' one of them said.

It was true that if you pressed your forehead against the window, you could see a mountain that may or may not have been Mont Blanc.

59

In Switzerland the landscape was not mixed up in my problems yet. We sat by the lake and threw pebbles in and watched the Swiss strolling leisurely around, reconciling earth and money. Some of them stripped down to their silk underwear, waded into the water and swam amongst the swans.

'Let's move to Switzerland,' one of the kids said one afternoon.

I had almost forgotten how we got there in the first place. That night with Maurice had acquired a glossy sheen over it that made it look like a sort of painting when I thought about it – beautiful, still, possibly fictional. In Switzerland your actions in other countries were of such little consequence that it was unclear if they really mattered at all. I guessed my job didn't exist anymore. That was one way of dealing with it. It didn't require much imagination to consider that the house we lived in and the unmade beds and the unpaid bills didn't exist either.

60

I wondered how long we could go on like this – on the surface of the earth with nobody to notice us, talk to us, fall in love with us. The longest sentence that anybody uttered to me was to ask whether I would like cream in my coffee. The children and I had done a wonderful visionary job of planning the rest of our lives in a twin-bed hotel room on the surface of an expensive lakeside town.

Then I ran out of money.

Then my cellphone rang.

It was the children's father. That was what I called him now. He was interested to know where on earth we were.

61

There was no news of the Movement on the internet. There was news of melting glaciers and plastic in salt and multinational corporations' theatrical attempts at tax evasion and a plane that had been forced to land because a woman used her sleeping husband's thumb to unlock his phone, discovered his infidelity and became hysterical and violent. There was not even anything on our neighbourhood's online weekly gazette. I went to call Maurice to make sure I hadn't just imagined our work of the night. It would not be the first time. I'd once had an intense relationship with someone for six years and it was not until I messaged him, asking him when he would be coming to visit, that I was sick of living without him, that it became apparent that what had happened had not happened at all. He couldn't remember that day in the phone box, or that party where we'd walked from room to room to room until we found one that was empty, or the cornfield or the song or the lake. It turned out he was getting married the following week. Maurice hadn't recorded a message on his voicemail – I got a female robot who told me that 06 87 43 21 20 was currently unavailable. It was not until I began telling the robot who I was and that I was on my way back from Switzerland and could he call me ASAP that I realised I was at the bottom of the river.

62

The children and I got back late at night but there was no denying the fact that all the windscreens on our street were more transparent than they'd ever been. There was no trace of black. I'd remembered leaving a trace of spots like an extended ellipsis over the grey van on the corner, but the spots too were gone. There had been no author.

'Maybe it was a dream,' one of the children said.

'Maybe.'

I'd had too many dreams of this variety. I unlocked the door and the children surrendered to their euphoria at the sight of the familiar, and thundered up and down the stairs. For them it was a renaissance. I lingered in the kitchen, tidying up the breakfast things we'd left on the table in our hasty departure – the lidless plum jar, the stray cornflakes, crumbs and tea leaves. Where was I? At breakfast six days ago. How could everything you'd done be snatched away from you? It was worse than jetlag. Maybe it was disappointment. I'd misunderstood my impatience about returning and getting arrested. At least it would have been a way out.

My eldest child came down to tell me that something had changed. Her eyes were clean and bright in the greasy kitchen light. I asked her what she meant.

'I don't know,' she said again. 'Everything just feels different.'

I liked her right then. She was like an angel coaxing me on, trying to get me to believe.

63

I took someone's place just after we got back. Her name was
Madame Conquet. She'd fainted on her second day back and
I'd been sent in to replace her. I found out various things
about her. People enjoyed describing her to me whenever an
opportunity arose. She was very brilliant; she was very tall;
she had very long legs; she didn't eat lunch; she was very nice;
she had anorexia; she needed help; she was a disaster; she
had blonde eyelashes; she didn't answer her phone; she'd got
top marks from that elite university she'd been to; she didn't
return messages; she was clearly incompetent. They looked
me up and down, fascinated by the new form she'd taken,
looking at me as you look at someone that's just walked out
of the hairdresser's, compelled to verbalise the differences –
the curly hair instead of the straight, the natural look instead
of the heavy eyeliner, the slightly shorter aspect, or was it just
those high heels that she wore – while studying my eyes for
flickers of the person I had replaced. In the beginning, I used
my own name. I couldn't tell whether it was the pronunciation
or my obscurity as a person that was problematic, but once
I had clarified that I was replacing Madame Conquet others
were able to relax around me. After several weeks I found
these introductions long-winded and exhausting. It seemed
more efficient to pare it back to the essentials.

'I'm replacing Madame Conquet,' I began to say before they could ask. These four words came as a relief to everyone. They were much happier with this small adjustment. I had given them all they needed to know and no more. They nodded approvingly at my editorial skills and went about their business at the photocopy machine. Now that they knew who I really was, they enjoyed introducing me to others who happened to walk into the room.

'This is Madame Conquet's replacement,' they said, and offered to buy me a coffee from the coffee machine.

'Madame Conquet always liked a cappuccino.'

They were pleased when, like Madame Conquet, I didn't take two sugars or even one. I wasn't used to milk in my coffee but I grew to like the synthetic creaminess of powdered milk, almost, and the smattering of cocoa that reminded me of the time just before I turned eleven. It wasn't long before I went from being Madame Conquet's replacement to just Madame Conquet. It was a busy place. Why not do away with the unnecessary syllables?

64

I was possibly my mother. That would make sense. Colleagues mentioned bruises on the upper arm area. I'd always had a weakness for singlets. How on earth had I hunted down the same man she'd married? It was preposterous and incredible, magical and mythological. I'd gone to great lengths to find him in an obscure village 18,972 kilometres from my hometown. It was fun in the beginning, when there was the illusion that I was writing a new story. Then it became apparent the story had already been written. I was tracing the letters like those French school children in their French notebooks, careful to make sure my *r*'s went no higher than absolutely necessary. That would explain why the chapters kept going, why natural endings became denaturalised. I made some tea and sat back with the crossword puzzle. There would of course be an ending; I just had to wait for it. There was something funny about becoming the star of stories you'd only heard about before. Did you really just tell the neighbours you'd fallen off your bike, causing your cheek to hit a fire hydrant? It was even funnier when they believed you. Some people enjoyed hearing the same story over and over. This was not to say I didn't try. I paid a babysitter and put on some red lipstick and black jeans and went out looking for an exit while he was away. Endings still belonged to other people, it seemed.

65

The claustrophobia increased as we made our way to the shortest day. The Movement had entered a dormant phase. Although nothing was happening on the street I could feel its furtive developments as it travelled deeper inward. I could feel Hélène's influence in the sensation of careful unstitching. What was identity except a bit of knitting? In a way I was grateful for the bruises, the way they numbed who I thought I was. My son salvaged the stick insect faeces from the classroom insectarium, claiming that they were eggs. He told me that the eggs looked just like the faeces but that he alone had learnt to tell the difference. I nodded liberally. That was the kind of mother I was. The faeces lived with some creeper leaves in a Tupperware box on top of the piano. We were supposed to spray the leaves with water every day. We did it the first day. After five months I suggested transferring the contents of the box to the garden. Then when the eggs hatched they would be very happy to find themselves in their natural environment. Plus, the box was beginning to smell.

'No,' my son said.

The box got moved around to different hiding places. I spilled cold tea on it once. The creeper grew dehydrated-looking, autumnal. For a while the box lived on top of the washing machine until my son found it and put it back on top of the piano. I moved it upstairs to his room. He brought it back down again. I put it in the hot-water cupboard. One Tuesday morning, as I hunted for my cheque book under the pile of drawings and bills stacked on the piano, I noticed a tiny stick on the side of the box. It was swaying back and forth on legs that were almost invisible.

66

I got a phone call from the consultant from Kerala saying he would be passing through. He looked fat and awkward against the slim French landscape. We met on the corner of two busy streets and I could see he was also surprised by my appearance, but perhaps it was just my dress – the flowers on it were intensely red. It was hard to tell if we were different people or if the spring light was showing up aspects of our characters that had been shadowed during the other part of the year, but the conversation was sluggish. This had never been a problem for us before. He persisted, and held my hand under the table – something he'd always gone out of his way to avoid. He admired my black eye. I too was pleased with the result. I'd spent all afternoon finding the right shade so I could make both eyes match.

'Midnight blue,' I told him.

'I was just wondering if you were happy,' he said.

The question annoyed me and I got up to go to the bathroom. My period was five days late and it was making me restless. When I came back he was stirring sugar into an elaborate hot chocolate.

'Look at this, isn't this the most beautiful thing you've ever seen?'

'Not really.'

I didn't mean the words to weigh so much. They lay between us like a squirming baby waiting to be picked up. He kept studying the perfect swirls of cream on his hot chocolate so he wouldn't have to look at me. The other people at the café had many things to say to each other. Should they invite Jean-Yves for dinner or not? It was just that he never even brought a bottle of wine. What time was the movie on tonight? Should they see it or should they not? Or should they see the one about the two colleagues who realise they are having the same dream? What else did they need to pick up on the way home? Some milk and green peppercorns for the beef salad. Was Ariane going to meet them here or at the party later? It was possible she wasn't going to come at all because she didn't want to run into Thierry, and Luke had told her he would be there. We used to say things like this to each other. He started nibbling his bottom lip like someone about to jump. Then he got cold feet and sipped his hot chocolate. We walked out of the café together and went our separate ways at the corner.

67

Time turned cheap and I was careless with it, squandering the morning away on half a piece of toast. Sometimes I glanced at the articles I was sent – 'Tracing the anaemic stellar halo of M101' – but it was difficult to concentrate on the dense paragraphs and milky titles. There were too many stars. I was lost without the pollution. Before, I could find my way between the Southern Cross and the Archer. Now it was just a big mess.

I called Juliette and asked her a few questions.

'I think I might be turning into a tree,' I said. She thought this was funny.

'How's Romeo?' I said. 'Did you get rid of him yet?'

'No,' she said in a way that told me he was in the room with her. There were a few beats while we waited for him to leave.

'I want to, but you know how it is when you're in love with someone.'

She sounded like she was eating toasted muesli. I wondered if she'd used the right word. (*Love: fondness combined with sexual attraction.*) But I was interested.

'How is it?'

'Um.' Another spoonful of muesli.

Then she said, 'Horrible. Excruciating.'

She said this like there was an actual bleeding wound on her leg that had been freshly sprayed with disinfectant. I wondered if she was going to cry. I hunted for something other than the relentless blue out the window. A wisp of white would have been something. Her voice changed into that of a professional as she began answering questions I hadn't asked.

'No, I can't. Yes, it's just that. I don't work that day,' so that I could hear that he had walked back into the room. She had suddenly lost her appetite.

68

Letters turned up on my desk addressed to Madame Conquet. I tried taking them back but the secretary who distributed the mail told me I should open them in case they concerned me. She told me that as far as the administration was concerned she and I were the same person. Madame Conquet had an overdue library book called 365 *Quotes and Aphorisms* and was on a union mailing list. They sent regular letters detailing employees' rights. I sometimes sat down and read the letters on my coffee break. I got a second and a third overdue notice, and then ten days later a letter came saying I owed the library twenty-nine euros. I kept all the letters in a purple folder on my desk, ready to hand over to her when she came back. I only had three weeks left in my three-month contract but I grew antsy – this was not the sort of job I'd ever wanted to do. I'd never wanted to work in an office. This was not who I was. I didn't even own a library card. My boss called me into his office the week my contract was due to end and told me he'd talked to Madame Conquet that morning and she was not at all fit to come back to work yet. My contract had been extended; my duties would be continued for another three months. I noticed how artfully he used the passive voice. I went back to my desk and tried to scratch off the white sticky labels she'd stuck onto her ballpoint pens. They left a gummy residue all over my fingers but I got most of them off. I wondered what Madame Conquet did all day, now that I had taken over her duties — if she read books and translated articles and went for long walks, as I had once done; if she lay around on the couch eating breakfast for dinner and was on the jury of an East European film festival; if she went rock-climbing and had sex sometimes with the guy that worked there in the mornings; if she played the flute and ate half a grapefruit for lunch; if she now had time to read more than one aphorism a day. The letters started coming thick and fast and I got into a ridiculous state. I couldn't stand the sight of them anymore. In the end I paid the twenty-nine euros. For a moment I felt as if I were finally taking my own life into my hands.

69

I found myself on a beach in Thailand. It was not a destination I personally would have chosen. There were many other people like me there, juxtaposed onto the picturesque landscape in different-coloured bikinis, their backs and shoulders various hues of red. They too seemed to have lost sight of why they were there. There was something robotic in their movements as they navigated their way between the pool and the loungers and the breakfast buffet, their limbs moving in a way that appeared rote-learned rather than spontaneous. They gravitated towards the pool after breakfast, favouring certain loungers over others, although they were all the same. Every now and then their mouths moved, words coming out in languages which, over the days I was there, merged into the same global message. I listened to a father and son conversing incomprehensibly one morning as they sucked pale yellow drinks through plastic straws, and it was only when the son stood up and said, 'Fuck you, Dad, you fucking asshole,' raising his voice slightly, that I realised they were speaking English. People approached Thai sellers on the beach and automatically began interrogating them, rattling off in their various languages what might have been questions, as if they were unable to tell the difference between a robot and a human being.

70

I was woken one night by gleeful French voices yelling from the pool just below my window. Although I had grown used to the blur of languages, I recognised the sensation of claustrophobia the sound of this particular language set off in me, and I got up to look at the new arrivals jumping and shouting and laughing in the tropical rain. Some of them were taking their clothes off as if to exhibit their humanity, the male sexual organs flopping around as they ran. People often started off clearly defined like this. For the first day or two they imposed themselves on their surroundings, but by days three or four they had grown paler and quieter as the landscape grew around and over them. The rain was abundant and the lush greenery flourished. And then one day they disappeared altogether. There was usually someone else to replace their spot on the loungers they had left behind.

71

I heard that the sun was halfway through its lifetime, that it was about as old as me. In another four billion years it would be dead. The sun and I grew closer. In the mornings I lay in the small triangle it left in the corner of the room, feeling it creep away from me like love. I missed Maurice's friend. I thought that I might run into him in Thailand. If I'd found out his name I could have tracked him down on Facebook. Then he would have been my friend instead of Maurice's. But now we could never be friends. We would wander Facebookless around the universe like exiles.

It was okay. There were other people you could believe in. I bought a lightweight crucifix in a second-hand shop and wore it over my shirt where everyone could see it. It had a small fake diamond for a heart. The pink-haired shop owner told me it had once belonged to a great believer. It was unclear whether it was the believer or the belief that no longer existed. I walked up a hill to the chapel. Other believers had left bunches of artificial flowers on the altar where they would never wilt. I sat on the single pew and waited, and when nothing happened I pulled on the long rope that hung down over the doorway and listened to the bells.

72

Someone came to talk to me about the cycle of violence. She was understanding about my lack of personality, and made herself a cup of tea in the kitchen, dunking the same milky teabag in a second cup of hot water which she then handed to me. She said there were four phases: tension building, violence, honeymoon and calm, and asked me whether these sounded familiar. I said that they sounded like the phases of the menstrual cycle.

She got angry at me for making such a stupid remark and some of the tea splashed out of her cup as she spoke. Did I really think that females were biologically bound into violence? That they were destined to repetitive abuse because they had babies? How could I possibly draw a parallel between a healthy bodily function and an absolutely unnecessary violent relationship? Did I think that there was no way out? Was I aware that this was the kind of thinking that was so damaging to women? Did I think I deserved it? How could I view the menstrual cycle in such negative terms?

I didn't know which question to answer first.

I handed her a spotty tea-towel to wipe the tea off her blouse.

I told her I didn't believe any of those things – I was just observing a certain resemblance in my own cycle. I sipped my tea, which tasted second-hand.

'I think that is exactly what you do believe,' she said, eyeing my crucifix with her small blue eyes, keeping both her hands around her mug this time when she spoke.

'I must say,' she said, 'it's a surprising vision of the world for a child of Christ to have.'

She had regained her professional calm and her sips were now controlled and regular. She looked a bit like someone else I knew. I didn't want to tell her, in case she got angry again with me for thinking that one thing was like another thing. She reminded me of my midwife. She was not at all like her, but at the same time it was her all right, sitting there waiting for me to hurry up and get on with it. It wasn't the first time I'd noticed that people you once knew could turn up again. She stood up and told me she was going to go now, that it was getting late and she had someone else to see. She'd be back to see me soon. It was clear that I wasn't ready to help myself yet. She took her cup into the kitchen and rinsed it. My midwife had done that too – not the cup; she'd always left hers on the table with a puddle of milky tea at the bottom – she'd also told me she was leaving despite the fact that I'd asked her to come over because I was in labour. She'd told me that the contractions I was feeling weren't contractions at all.

73

When I had the crucifix on, people were gentler, kinder. They stepped carefully around me as if I were a little broken or old. I was wearing it the day I crossed paths with the middle-aged chain-smoker. He was not wearing his cape that day. I sat at the café table next to his and waited for him to save me. While I was waiting I eavesdropped on his conversation with a man who could have been his brother. Waitresses now called him David, which reminded me of Goliath, although I could remember nothing about the story except that he was the youngest of twelve brothers. David had just finished writing two hundred pages of his book. He had so many things to think about. He felt close to the end, but at the same time he knew he had a long way to go. He got up to saunter around the café in his big unlaced boots, confidence rising from their soles. When he came back to the table he had more things to say. Walking had dislodged new adjectives and visions. How could anyone be pinned down to a single identity, to a name? He was not at all who most people thought he was.

I got up to go to the bathroom – I felt the need to get away from him. In his presence I was having trouble recognising the emotion he had stirred in me, which was making me feel sweaty and cold. Being around him was like being in another country: I wanted to get out, and once I was out I wished I were back in.

74

There was a framed map of the world in the bathroom and I couldn't help noticing the area of pale blue sea that had replaced the place I was born. Leaning in closer, I saw there were a few pale squiggles as if the whole place had been swallowed up by the benevolent-looking sea, and this was the foamy evidence that such a country had ever existed at all. Perhaps it was a map ahead of its time, which had already factored in the countries that, in a thousand years or so, would no longer be visible on the surface of the earth. Although this didn't explain why islands such as Tahiti still boasted such a clear outline. The prime minister of my country had recently made a statement about this worrying phenomenon of missing countries, which was quite inexplicable; how (on earth) could so many maps fail to include clearly existent countries? It was not fair, she said. She wouldn't stand for it.

I wound my way back through the chairs and tables that had been set for lunch. Although it was only eleven thirty there was already a group of people sipping flutes of champagne, the grey roots of their hair sprouting out of their scalps, threatening to boycott the corporate black of their costumes. There was a chair at the table that might have been for me. I sat in it, just to see if transplanting a life could be a straightforward operation after all. That put an end to their light banter. The woman in the purple jumpsuit took a nervous sip from her glass.

'Madame Hours-Kannoussi?' a man with a trim ginger beard enquired. He could have played Shakespeare in a biographical television drama. He was clearly more used to people not conforming to how he'd imagined them than his colleagues were, although my long flowing dress and crucifix brought some doubt into his voice.

'Yes?'

There was a communal lowering of eyes, which I appreciated, something holy about the gesture.

David had not witnessed this little digression, which I was half disappointed about. It was clearly a ploy for attention. He was standing at the counter trying to make all the twenty-centime coins in his pocket add up to the price of a coffee. I admired his good posture and strong back. I stood next to him at the counter, close enough to smell the scent of damp trees on him, and began to pray. He was making beautiful piles of gold coins all over the counter. I was trying to remember how it went with superheroes – you couldn't just go up to them and say, 'I know who you are.' I thought most of them were endowed with powerful vision, but when he finished counting all his coins, he turned and strode right past me.

77

I went to church on the way home. It hadn't changed much since I was a kid. It was the same dismal place it had always been. I had never understood what they had against windows. I walked in on the middle of a hymn. I glanced around at the other believers, most of whom were doing a bad job of miming the words. The organ was efficient, however, at drowning out any discrepancies. I sat next to a man in a blue suit who was eager to share his songbook with me, but I didn't feel like singing. I closed my eyes and he quickly got the message. Prayer overrules everything else. I remembered that lesson from Sunday school.

I was interrupted by a patting on the shoulder from my blue-suited neighbour; he pointed to the short queue that was forming in the aisle. Communion never used to come around so fast. We were good friends by now and he let me go ahead of him. There was just the mild smell of rotten corn that came out of his mouth when he talked, but I felt quite close to him when he was behind me. There was subdued excitement in the air as the believers stretched their legs; this, along with the post-service morning tea, was one of the high moments. Could there be anything better than putting the blood and body of the imaginary in one's mouth? It was an old childhood trick that we'd all enjoyed playing. Bored with our sedentary roles, my brother and I had gravitated into the vestry while the others were rehearsing the Christmas story. I was the star that the wise men followed and my only task was to stand very still, and my brother was one of many sheep. Our Sunday School teacher had not liked my idea that the star should suddenly die and explode into a million baby stars. She said that we were here to depict what had happened, not what might have happened.

We had hoped it would be harder to find the sacred box of rice wafers. We ate so much of Christ's body that we experienced an extreme spiritual high that sent us running around in hallucinatory circles. My brother had never understood how someone's body could be so tasteless. He got bad indigestion later and my mother had to give him some antacids.

I got down on my knees with the others. The bald priest was not holding a silver plate of wafers this time but a large loaf of stale-looking bread that he was tearing chunks out of. A French touch, I suppose. Anything could be holy with enough blessing. The words were the same.

This is my body which is given for you. Do this in remembrance of me.

I closed my eyes and held out my hands, waiting for the stranger's index finger to etch a cross into my head. His was more of a caress, although he came back with three small hard punctuations where the nails went. I washed the stale bread down with the cheap wine and tried to remember something.

78

My new friend didn't have to twist my arm too hard to get me into the back room for morning tea afterwards. This I also remembered as one of the highlights. And it was the same evocative smell, like at the dentist's. It was always refreshing to see a priest relaxing with a chocolate biscuit. The man in blue and I talked straight through three instant coffee refills – there was a believer that kept coming round with a thermos and filling up our cups, like on the plane; it was some technique to prolong our presence in the small room with peeling wallpaper.

The man in blue liked to describe his dead wife in detail, offering different parts of her body and personality and habits up to me, interspersing them throughout our conversation so that I was left with a sort of cubist sketch of her at the end. I interrupted him when he started in again with her distinctive grey eyes. I said there was someone I knew on the other side of the room. This just happened to be true. It was John, my friend who lived in a caravan. I hadn't seen him in the service, I said.

'No,' he said. He told me he came here every Sunday and Thursday for the tea and biscuits. They usually had better ones – last week there had been these caramel and chocolate ones with sprinkles on top. They even had sausage rolls sometimes. And there was also a cupboard they opened up at the end with clothes you could choose from. He'd got some of his best clothes here – he'd picked up an Yves Saint Laurent shirt last week. He wouldn't come here otherwise. He'd been raised by a bunch of nuns and couldn't stand the smell of them. He held his cup steady while the believer filled his cup.

79

Sometimes I followed David around. He liked to pretend he couldn't see me. He was talented at it and could look straight through me without flinching. At first I was worried, but I saw him doodling pictures of me in his notebook. He quickly tried to flip over the pages, but my reflexes were faster than his. I was reminded of Fussa. My mother had to scrub off the portraits I had left of her all over my bedroom wall when she finally left my father.

It was unclear where David was going. He was as intent as the rest of us on being special. He'd stride off down the street and suddenly disappear. He drank a lot of black coffee. He pulled his hair up in a top-knot like Māui. Once I saw him carrying a ladder and I followed him down into the metro. He was wearing his cape that day and it was easier to keep track of him. I liked following him; it gave purpose to my life. He always looked so driven, as if there were a place he was actually going. He got off the metro three stops later and I stood next to him at the lights, waiting for the red man to turn into a green one. I followed him for two blocks, slowing as he slowed. We approached a grey building with red shutters. All that transubstantiated bread inside me was giving me someone else's personality, and I followed him in. Unfortunately, there were two doors and I was not fast enough to catch the second one before it locked shut. His cape disappeared up the wooden stairs. There was a door code and I tried several different combinations of my birth date before giving up. There was a café next door at which people sat waiting, and I waited with them until I couldn't wait any longer. I had to pick up the kids at four.

80

Why couldn't getting out mean going out the way you came in? There were signs that indicated I was getting closer to childhood. I picked daisies in my spare time. The pleasure of small sweets that fizzed into oblivion on your tongue. My dirty feet. The distraction of other things. There were unfinished projects scattered all over the floor that people told me were mine. 'Why can't you finish anything you start?' I was asked several times. But I couldn't answer. I couldn't think of anything to say to the adults at the dinner party. I could barely understand what they were saying. I sat on the uncomfortable chair and grew smaller and smaller until it was time for dessert.

'What?' I said on the odd occasions I was asked a direct question. I was usually able to give a syllable or two the second time around. Unsure of what else to do with me, they patted me on the head and rubbed me on the arm to make sure I was still there. I picked up someone's baby and went to play with him in the garden.

My personality turned soft and pliable and the children's father became worried that he didn't know who I was anymore. It turned out to be harder to hurt someone whose personality kept turning blank. I could feel the insect in me as I adapted to my environment. I believed in superheroes.

I developed a liking for T-shirts with slogans on them and wrote them all down in my notebook.

Memories Don't Die.

Save the Whales.

I Can and I Will.

I got out the pile of *Disinvent Yourself* T-shirts I kept at the back of my drawer. I couldn't remember why we'd ordered so many extra-large ones. I wore a clean one every day. There were so many left over that I could get through a whole month without washing any of them.

81

The thunder woke me. I had been happily living my life out in a small town by the sea. The houses had all had red and orange roofs. I had been walking to the top of a hill. There was a sandwich in my backpack that I was going to eat once I got to the top of the hill, because I was hungry – my stomach had growled, softly at first, then wildly like an animal or the world ending, which I guess it was. Here I was in a double bed in a room in a big city. The thunder growled again, close enough to make the house tremor. My heart was still beating fast from the exertion up the hill. There was an almost naked man next to me. He was not exactly snoring. I closed my eyes in an attempt to return to the walk, my carefully made sandwich, the satisfaction of small things; I was supposed to be meeting somebody at the top of the hill, but I might as well have been trying to wedge myself back up the vaginal canal. I kicked off the duvet and listened to the rain, which fell suddenly.

Notes

Page 5: The quote that appears as an epigraph is from Abdullah Öcalan's book *Democratic Confederalism*, translated by the International Initiative (London: Transmedia Publishing, 2011), p. 25. freeocalan.org/books/#/book/democratic-confederalism

Page 36: The song by Jacques Brel is 'Ne me quitte pas' (1959).

Page 40: The 'French rock star' refers to the singer of the band Noir Désir. The song alluded to is 'Le vent nous emportera' (2001).

Pages 42–43: These pages contain several references to Abdullah Öcalan's life and work. The quote is from his book *Liberating Life: Women's Revolution*, translated by the International Initiative (London: Transmedia Publishing, 2013), p. 14. http://freeocalan.org/books/#/book/liberating-life-womans-revolution

Page 47: A slightly different version of this section first appeared in *Landfall* 238 (November 2019).

Page 68: This section first appeared as a Friday Poem on *The Spinoff*.

Acknowledgements

Thank you,

Ashleigh Young,

Fergus Barrowman and everyone at VUP,

Bernadette Hall,

Roger Steele,

Abigael, Gabriel, Jeanne, Olivier,

and the whānau.